Hiya! My name Thudd. Best robot friend of Drewd. Thudd know lots of stuff. How bug walk up wall. Why bubble break. How spider make web!

Drewd like to invent stuff. Thudd help! But sometime Thudd and Drewd make mistake. Invention plus mistake make adventure! Thudd and Drewd go on adventure now. Want to come? Turn page, please!

Get lost with
Andrew, Judy, and Thudd
in all their exciting adventures!

*Andrew Lost on the Dog*
*Andrew Lost in the Bathroom*
*Andrew Lost in the Kitchen*
*Andrew Lost in the Garden*

AND COMING SOON!
*Andrew Lost Under Water*

# ANDREW LOST

**4**

## IN THE GARDEN

BY J. C. GREENBURG

ILLUSTRATED
BY DEBBIE PALEN

A STEPPING STONE BOOK™

Random House 🏠 New York

*To Dan and Zack and Dad*
*and the real Andrew, with love.*
*—J.C.G.*

*To Barb, my mother, for her*
*love of gardening.*
*—D.P.*

www.randomhouse.com/kids
www.AndrewLost.com

*Library of Congress Cataloging-in-Publication Data*
Greenburg, J. C. (Judith C.)
In the garden / by J. C. Greenburg ; illustrated by Debbie Palen.
  p.   cm. — (Andrew Lost ; 4)
"A stepping stone book."
SUMMARY: Andrew, his cousin Judy, and Thudd the robot, having been shrunk by a shrinking machine, encounter many terrifying creatures, including Mrs. Scuttle, as they try to reach the Atom Sucker before it explodes.
ISBN 0-375-81280-6 (trade) — ISBN 0-375-91280-0 (lib. bdg.)
[1. Inventions—Fiction. 2. Insects—Fiction. 3. Invertebrates—Fiction. 4. Size—Fiction. 5. Cousins—Fiction.]   I. Palen, Debbie, ill. II. Title.
PZ7.G82785 Io 2003   [Fic]—dc21   2002014972

Printed in the United States of America
First Edition  10 9 8 7 6 5 4 3 2 1

# ANDREW'S WORLD

**Andrew Dubble**

Andrew is ten years old, but he's been inventing things since he was four! His newest invention is the Atom Sucker. It shrinks things by sucking the space out of their atoms.

At noon today, Andrew shrunk himself, his robot Thudd, and his cousin Judy. Now they're so small, they could play baseball on the head of a pin. If they don't get back to the Atom Sucker by eight o'clock, they'll be small forever!

## Judy Dubble

Judy is Andrew's thirteen-year-old cousin. She's pretty annoyed at Andrew. Since he shrunk them, she's been snuffled into a dog's nose, flushed down a toilet, and buttered on a slice of toast. But Andrew shrunk her parents' helicopter, too. If they can find it, she can fly them back to the Atom Sucker. But they've got only two hours before the Atom Sucker explodes!

## Thudd

Thudd is a little silver robot and Andrew's best friend. The letters in his name stand for The Handy Ultra-Digital Detective.

Thudd has a super-computer brain and knows almost everything. Thanks to Thudd, Uncle Al is on the way!

## Uncle Al

Alfred Dubble is Andrew and Judy's uncle.

He's a top-secret scientist. He invented Thudd!

Uncle Al wants to help Andrew and Judy and Thudd get unshrunk. But there's no way he can get there before eight o'clock!

## Harley

Harley is a basset hound. He belongs to Judy's neighbor Mrs. Scuttle, but Judy is his best friend.

Judy thought she saw her parents' helicopter in Harley's ear. But Andrew and Judy are buzzing over the garden on the back of a fly. How are they going to get off the fly and back onto Harley?

## Mrs. Scuttle

Mrs. Scuttle is Judy's next-door neighbor. Harley belongs to her. Mrs. Scuttle is getting ready for a garden party. The Atom Sucker is getting ready to blow up!

# 1 THE BIG BUZZ

*I guess you should never count on a bug to solve your problems,* thought Andrew Dubble as he flew above the garden on the back of a fly.

*Bzzzzzzzz . . .*

The fly wings behind him buzzed like a noisy engine. The wind whooshed against his face.

Next to Andrew was his thirteen-year-old cousin, Judy. She was clinging to a hair behind one of the fly's huge black eyes. Andrew's little silver robot, Thudd, was hanging tight to the same hair as Andrew.

A few minutes ago, they'd almost become part of an afternoon snack for Judy's neighbor Mrs. Scuttle. But just in time, they'd managed to flee on the fly. Now they were zooming above Mrs. Scuttle's garden.

*Kraaaack!*

Mrs. Scuttle's screen door slammed.

"Disgusting fly!" yelled Mrs. Scuttle. She ran from the kitchen waving a yellow fly swatter. "I'll get you!"

Below them, Andrew and Judy could see a brick path. It led from Mrs. Scuttle's kitchen door to a cement patio with a picnic table.

All around the path was Mrs. Scuttle's garden. Purple daisies and pink lilies waved in the breeze. Rosebushes grew next to a white fence that separated Mrs. Scuttle's yard from Judy's.

"Look!" said Judy, pointing to her yard. "I can see your stupid Atom Sucker!"

The Atom Sucker was Andrew's latest

invention. At noon today, it had shrunk them so small they could take a hike on the head of a pin.

To get unshrunk, they had to get back to the Atom Sucker by 8:01, before it blew up!

Andrew and Judy felt a gust of wind as Mrs. Scuttle's fly swatter swished by them. The fly flew in dizzy circles to get away.

Floating through the air were things that looked like spiky Ping-Pong balls. Some of them got stuck in Judy's long, frizzy hair.

*meep* . . . "Pollen!" squeaked Thudd. "From flowers! Make baby plants."

"Oh, *great*!" said Judy, trying to pull the sticky things out of her hair. "I'm allergic to pollen! Ah . . . ah . . . ahhhhh . . . *chooof!*"

The fly swatter was right above them when Mrs. Scuttle let out a scream.

"Harley, *noooo!*"

Harley was Mrs. Scuttle's basset hound. He was standing next to the white fence. He was raising his leg!

Suddenly Andrew felt his stomach fluttering up to his mouth. The fly was going into a dive! The wind rushed against his face so hard he could barely keep his eyes open. The garden turned into a green blur.

Andrew and Judy almost flew off the fly as it landed in the dirt. Their noses filled with strange moldy smells. On one side of the fly was a huge leaf bristling with hairs. On the other side was the brick path.

The fly crept along the ground. It stopped in front of a pile of shiny black goo and unrolled a fat hose from below its eyes. It dipped the hose into the goo.

*meep* . . . "Fly eating!" said Thudd.

"What's it eating?" asked Judy.

*meep* . . . "Oody not want to know," said Thudd.

"Yes I *do*," said Judy.

*meep* . . . "Bug poop!" said Thudd.

"*Eeeeew!*" said Judy. "Let's ditch this yucky bug!"

She started unwrapping the stretchy strands of Drastic Elastic that Andrew had used to hold them on the fly. It was another one of Andrew's inventions.

"Don't tangle the Drastic Elastic," said Andrew. "We might need it later."

Judy finished unwrapping herself and handed the long loops of Drastic Elastic to Andrew. He snapped it like a yo-yo, and it shrank drastically. It was only as long as one of Andrew's fingers!

Andrew tucked the Drastic Elastic into the secret pocket under his shirt collar. He zipped the pocket closed.

"I'm out of here!" said Judy, sliding down from behind the fly's eye. Andrew followed her. Since they were as light as dust, they floated gently down.

Suddenly a scream rattled Andrew's ears.

"Cheese Louise!" Judy hollered. "This is more disgusting than when we were flushed down the toilet!"

# BEAR-LY THERE

Andrew landed next to Judy. He landed on something squishy! It was a transparent blob. And it was squirming!

As far as Andrew could see, blobs and globs were wriggling over chunks of damp brown dirt!

There were blobs that looked like hairy party balloons with mouths!

There were globs shaped like rubbery pancakes that folded and flopped along.

Wormy things wiggled over the others.

*meep* . . . "Lotsa little guys live in dirt,"

said Thudd. "Billions! Eat germs and dead stuff. Recycle stuff. Make food for plants!"

"Look at this one!" said Andrew. He pointed to something shaped like a hairy basketball with a mouth. It was as clear as a plastic sandwich bag. In the middle, there was a much smaller, pillow-shaped creature tumbling around.

Judy's eyes got wide. "I think this guy's lunch is still *alive!*"

As Andrew bent over to get a better look, something whacked him from behind.

"Oofers!" Andrew yelled.

"Eeeek!" screamed Thudd.

A black tentacle, long and fat and gummy, whipped around Andrew's chest. Parts of the tentacle puffed up like beach balls!

The tentacle got tighter and tighter. Andrew could hardly breathe!

*THWUNK!*

Suddenly the tentacle started to go

squishy! Thick yellow goo oozed out all over Andrew! The tentacle let go.

"Woofers!" said Andrew, catching his breath. He turned around.

Judy wagged her ballpoint pen in front of Andrew's face. It was dripping with tentacle goo.

"You owe me *big*-time, Bug-Brain," she said. "I just saved your annoying life!"

"Thudd, are you okay?" asked Andrew, reaching into his pocket.

*meep* . . . "Okey-dokey!" said Thudd as Andrew wiped goo off of him. "Drewd caught by noose fungus! Noose fungus catch tiny worms. Squash 'em! Eat 'em!"

Judy shook her head as she cleaned off her pen. "Fungus, shmungus. The only good fungus is a mushroom on a pizza."

Just then, Thudd's antennas started to wag. Thudd pointed to a bushy clump of moss under the giant leaf.

*meep* . . . "Want to go *there,* please!" he squeaked.

"Okay, Thudd," said Andrew, surprised. He had never seen Thudd so excited.

Andrew started toward the moss.

"Hey, wait a minute!" said Judy. "Before we do anything else, we need a plan. We've got to get to the helicopter."

Judy's parents kept a helicopter for their adventure-travel business. The helicopter got shrunk when Andrew and Judy did. Judy was sure she could fly it back to the Atom Sucker—if they could find it.

Judy tugged at a grain of pollen tangled in her hair. "I'm pretty sure it's stuck inside Harley's ear," she said. "The problem is, how do we get there?"

Thudd's antennas waggled toward the moss.

*meep* . . . "Think better over there," Thudd said.

Judy groaned. "Oh, all right!"

They hiked toward the moss. Every speck of dirt was as big as a boulder and covered with squirmy things.

When they got closer to the moss, they could see drops of water caught between the dark green leaves.

*meep* . . . "There!" said Thudd, pointing to a water drop.

Thudd pinched his way up Andrew's shirt and crept onto his shoulder.

Andrew looked into the drop. It was like looking into a huge fishbowl. There was something moving inside!

It looked like a chubby bear with eight legs and no hair. It was bigger than Andrew. It paddled toward the front of the water drop.

*meep* . . . "Want pet, please!" said Thudd.

"What *is* it?" asked Judy.

*meep* . . . "Water bear!" said Thudd. "Water bear special! If moss get dry, water

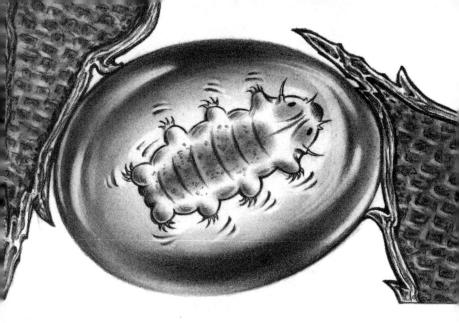

bear dry up, too. Not eat. Not drink. Can live for hundred years! Come back to life when moss get wet again. Good pet. Not need litter box! Want to take Spot home, please!"

"Spot?" said Andrew. He sighed. "We don't even know if we can *get* home."

Judy shook her head. "And look how big it is!"

Thudd sat down quietly on Andrew's shoulder.

Andrew thought for a moment. "How about this?" he said. "When we get back to normal, we can ask Uncle Al to come get Spot. Mrs. Scuttle likes Uncle Al."

"Good! Good! Good!" said Thudd. "Thunk oo!"

Thudd pressed a button on his chest. A thin yellow beam shot toward the water drop.

*meep* . . . "'Where's It?' beam find water bear again," said Thudd.

He waved to the water bear. Its little legs seemed to wave back.

As Thudd crept back into Andrew's pocket, they heard a sound like paper crinkling. Andrew turned.

A skyscraper-tall monster was standing behind them!

# 3 BUG-GOO, WHERE ARE YOU?

The monster's green legs seemed to go up for-ever. Way, way up, its front legs were folded.

At the top, its head was the shape of an upside-down triangle. Huge green eyes seemed to be staring down at them.

"It looks like those pictures of aliens," whispered Judy.

*meep* . . . "Praying mantis!" squeaked Thudd. "Praying mantis eat bugs. Even eat lizard!"

The mantis slowly raised a rear leg.

Judy shivered. "We're not big enough for

a praying mantis snack," she said. "But it could stomp us like a Tyrannosaurus."

"If only I had some Bug-Goo," said Andrew, digging through his shirt pockets.

"Bug-Goo!" said Judy. "Sounds like one of your stupid inventions. It better be bug repellent!"

Andrew looked away. "Um, actually, it smells like pizza to bugs," he said. "They'll come from miles away to get it."

"Super nutso!" said Judy. "You want the praying mantis to come and get *us*?"

Andrew unzipped a pocket on the leg of his shorts. Nothing was there. But at the back of that pocket was another pocket. Andrew felt a little lump. He pulled out a tiny plastic squirt bottle.

"Watch this," said Andrew.

He flipped the lid off the bottle and aimed behind the praying mantis. He gave a quick squeeze. One gloppy green drop of

Bug-Goo squirted out toward the shadowy leaves.

The mantis wagged its head. Its praying legs twitched. Then it turned and lurched toward the Bug-Goo!

"Look!" said Andrew.

Overhead, flies and bees and mosquitoes were zooming toward the Bug-Goo. Shiny brown beetles hopped off leaves and trudged toward the Bug-Goo, too.

Besides the buzzing of the bugs, there was another sound. It was coming from Judy's yard.

KAPOCKET . . . *kapocket kapocket* KAPOCKETA

It got louder.

*POCKETA . . . POCKETA POCKETA*

"What's that weird noise?" asked Judy.

"Uh-oh," said Andrew.

Judy glared at Andrew. "'Uh-oh' is *not* a good answer," she said.

"It could be the Atom Sucker," said

Andrew. "Um, it might mean it's getting kind of hot."

*Kraaaack!*

The screen door slammed. Mrs. Scuttle's giant feet clomped toward them in flip-flops.

Andrew and Judy looked up to see Mrs. Scuttle towing a bunch of colored balloons. A white banner trailed from her hand.

She went over to the fence and tied the balloons to it. She hung the banner between two trees. Big red letters said: HAPPY 5TH BIRTHDAY BOOT-A-PEST.

"Boot-a-Pest" was the name of Mrs. Scuttle's business. Boot-a-Pest got rid of bugs and anything else people didn't want living in their houses.

Mrs. Scuttle stepped back to take a look at her decorations. "Lovely!" she said. "This has been a terrible day, but I shall have a *perfect* garden party."

She turned around and clomped back

toward the kitchen door. One of her flip-flops almost flapped onto Andrew and Judy and Thudd!

Judy pointed to a leaf farther away from the path. "Let's climb onto that leaf before Mrs. Scuttle stomps us."

To get to the leaf, they had to climb over chunks of dirt the size of doghouses.

Dirt creatures tried to suck their feet. And the ground was a junkyard of other weird stuff.

Andrew stopped in front of something that looked like a piece of an orange wall. It was covered with scales, like the skin of a fish.

*meep* . . . "Butterfly wing," said Thudd, pointing to his face screen. "Bright orange color tell birds, 'Don't eat! Taste bad! Poison!'"

Andrew was looking toward the top of the wing when he saw something spinning down through the air. It was enormous! And it was spinning straight toward *them*!

"Run!" yelled Andrew.

# BIG GREEN LIPS

The thing thumped down right in front of them. It was huge and clear and hollow. It looked like a Jell-O mold of a blimp-sized bug!

*meep* . . . "Bug skeleton!" said Thudd.

Andrew touched it. "Feels like *plastic!*" he said.

FEELS LIKE PLASTIC!

*meep* . . . "Old skeleton from bug called cicada," said Thudd. "Bug grow. Get too big for skeleton. Grow new one."

Judy frowned. "I don't like the buzz-saw racket cicadas make on hot summer days," she said. "And these stupid bugs even made me lose a spelling bee!"

"Huh?" said Andrew.

Judy rolled her eyes. "I thought *cicada* started with an *s* because that's the way it sounds."

*meep* . . . "Seventeen years ago, lotsa this kinda cicada hatch from eggs," said Thudd. "Little cicadas dig deep into ground. Stay underground seventeen years! Suck tree roots. One night in June, cicadas crawl out of ground together!"

"After seventeen years, they all suddenly decide to come up at once?" asked Andrew.

"Yoop!" said Thudd. "Need safe place to get out of old skeleton. Crawl up tree. This

skeleton from cicada that come up early. Million cicadas coming up soon!"

"When?" asked Judy.

*meep* . . . "Tonight, maybe," said Thudd.

Judy shook her head. "So far today, we got snuffled up into a dog's nose, flushed down a toilet, and nearly melted onto a cheese-and-tomato sandwich. Now we could get trampled by a bug stampede!"

*Kraaaaaack!*

Mrs. Scuttle stomped out of the kitchen carrying a big white platter heaped high with sandwiches.

"Quick!" said Judy. "Get onto the leaf!"

The enormous leaf was touching the ground. Still, climbing onto it was like climbing a cliff.

Luckily, the leaf was covered with hairs. Judy grabbed one and pulled herself up. Andrew was right behind her.

"Cheese Louise!" shouted Judy. "This leaf's got lips!"

Andrew looked out over the leaf. It really *was* covered with lips. And they were all open!

*meep* . . . "Plant mouths," said Thudd. "Plant get food from air. Not eat *us*!"

Judy squinted at Thudd. "Are you sure?"

"Yoop!"

Judy and Andrew climbed farther onto the leaf.

Suddenly the big purple button in the middle of Thudd's chest started to blink.

"It's Uncle Al!" said Andrew.

Thudd's purple button popped open and a beam of purple light zoomed out.

Andrew and Judy sat down on the leaf.

"Hi guys!" said the hologram of their uncle Al. He was a little purple and they could see right through him. "Everyone okay?" he asked.

"We're sitting on plant lips!" said Judy.

"But they're pretty comfortable," said Andrew.

"You got yourselves into the garden!" said Uncle Al. "And my signal is reaching you

HI GUYS!

better. You must have stopped Thudd's antennas from rusting. You guys are really using your heads!"

"Uncle Al," said Judy. "We don't have much time left to get unshrunk."

*meep* . . . "7:25," said Thudd. "Thirty-six minutes till 8:01!"

"I'll be landing at the airport in thirty minutes," said Uncle Al. "But it will take ten minutes to get from the airport to you. Right now, I want you to think about the sign over my office door."

"Oh, yeah!" Andrew nodded. "It says, 'Questions have many answers.'"

"You've got it!" said Uncle Al. "It's the best magic I know. It works for anything. You can use it to make a pizza, find new planets, or get unshrunk!"

*sssssss*

There was static in Uncle Al's signal.

"I'm flying through some storm clouds,"

said Uncle Al. "My signal might cut out. But remember what I told—"

*sssssssSSSSSSSSSSSS*

The static grew louder, and Uncle Al disappeared.

*KAPOCKETA POCKETA POCKETA*
*KAPOCKETA POCKETA POCKETA*

"The Atom Sucker is getting louder," said Judy.

"Um, it could be getting hotter," said Andrew.

Thudd's antennas started to twitch.

*meep* . . . "Hear rumble," said Thudd. "Underground!"

Suddenly, in front of the leaf, a mountain of dirt popped up. A slimy brown torpedo shape poked through it!

# FEELING SHAKY

A long, bulgy thing was wiggling out. It looked like a Loch Ness Monster made of inner tubes.

*meep* . . . "Earthworm!" said Thudd.

"It's the size of a Brontosaurus!" said Judy. "I hope earthworms are vegetarians."

*meep* . . . "Earthworm swallow dirt," said Thudd. "Eat dead stuff and little dirt animals."

"Do you think it sees us?" asked Judy. "Maybe it thinks *we're* dirt snacks."

*meep* . . . "Earthworm not got eyes," said Thudd.

The front end of the worm wriggled toward their leaf. A patch of bright sunlight made the worm's damp skin look shiny.

*meep* . . . "Sun bad, bad, bad for worm," said Thudd. "If worm stay in sun, sun make poison inside worm skin. Worm die!"

"Then why is it coming out?" asked Andrew.

*meep* . . . "Worm feel stuff shake underground," said Thudd. "Maybe Atom Sucker noise make underground shake. Worm try to get away."

"I feel kind of sorry for him," said Judy.

*meep* . . . "Worm not 'him,'" said Thudd. "Worm not 'her.' Earthworm is male *and* female!"

"Hyper-weird!" said Judy. "What can we do to make it go back underground?"

"Maybe we can make a noise that will really annoy it," said Andrew. "Thudd knows every tune he's ever heard. He can even play the music. Thudd, do that song by Stinky Feet."

*meep* . . . "Worm not hear," said Thudd. "Worm just feel stuff shake when sound get loud."

"It's a loud song," said Andrew. "Maybe it's loud enough for the worm to feel it. Try it."

"Okey-dokey," said Thudd. He started to sing:

> *Dirty socks, dirty socks!*
> *They never clean,*
> *They make you mean.*
> *They start at toes,*
> *And then they goes*
> *From there*
> *Up to your hair!*

Thudd screamed the song as loudly as he could, but the worm kept coming. It lurched closer to their leaf.

Judy and Andrew scrambled to their feet. They stepped back without looking and accidentally stepped right off the leaf! They drifted down to the dirt.

*clip-clop . . . clip-clop . . . flap . . . flap . . . flap*

Sandals and sneakers were stomping along the brick path. Mrs. Scuttle's guests were arriving.

"Well, *hellooo*, Mrs. Snarfless!" they heard

Mrs. Scuttle say. "*Sooo* nice to see you. I'm sorry Mr. Snarfless can't be here. It's too bad about his toe problem. I hope they won't have to cut it off."

"Look what I got!" came the voice of a little boy.

"Jeremy Snarfless," said a woman's voice, "put that water gun down right now!"

Mrs. Scuttle clomped back to the kitchen. She had changed out of her flip-flops. Now she was wearing red sandals with high heels and bows on the front.

They heard Mrs. Scuttle mutter, "The invitation said 'no children.' She should have left that little rug rat home."

Andrew and Judy felt the ground shake as she stomped by.

The worm must have felt it, too. It stopped moving. Then, very slowly, it backed into its hole.

Thudd wagged his antennas.

*meep* . . . "Hear something."

"I just hear the Atom Sucker," said Judy.

*meep* . . . "Rustle, rustle," said Thudd.

Out of the corner of his eye, Andrew saw something move. He turned to see a dead brown leaf shivering. There was something oozing out from under it!

It looked like a yellow lake. And it was slithering toward them!

"Wait," said Judy. "I think I *do* hear something."

"It's probably just, um, a breeze," said Andrew. He didn't want Judy to get upset again. "But you look like you could use some exercise. Let's do some running."

Andrew took off.

# 6  ANT-ICIPATION

Judy took off after him. "Wait till I get my hands on you!" she yelled.

They climbed over a twig and tumbled down the side of a rock. They fell onto something that looked like a fluffy white cushion.

"Whew!" said Judy, catching her breath. "Let's rest here. So what was all that stupid running about?"

Andrew shrugged. "There was this humongous yellow ooze slithering toward us," he said.

*meep* . . . "Look!" Thudd pointed to his

face screen. "Slime mold is fungus village. Most of time, little fungus guys live alone. But when fungus guys run out of food, lotsa lotsa fungus guys get together. Make big ooze parade. Look for new place to eat."

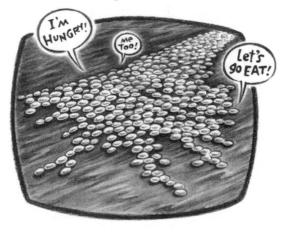

"Kind of like a class trip looking for lunch," said Andrew.

Judy frowned. "Great!" she said. "So will the slime follow us here?"

*meep* . . . "Slime mold not climb down rock," said Thudd.

"Good!" said Judy. She touched the fluffy

white strands of the thing they were sitting on. "This stuff is a little sticky, like cotton candy. But it's nice and comfy."

Andrew looked around the place they had fallen into. Suddenly his jaw dropped and his eyes got wide.

"Super-duper pooper-scooper!" shouted Andrew. He pointed to a mountain of dirt. "You know what that is?"

Judy rolled her eyes. "It's an anthill," she said. "But you'd better not be thinking what I think you're thinking. I don't want to hear one word about your antsy-schmancy science report."

"Judy, we've *got* to get into that anthill," said Andrew. "Now's our chance to find out incredible stuff!"

Judy shook her head. "After that ant sneaked up behind me on the sponge, I never want to see another ant again!"

"Aw, come on, Judy," Andrew pleaded.

"I think the ants are asleep now."

*meep* . . . "Ants not go beddy-bye yet," said Thudd.

"Don't *worry*," said Andrew. "You don't see any ants, do you?"

"Every time you say 'don't worry,'" said Judy, turning her back on Andrew, "an alarm goes off in my . . . *YIIIIIIKES!*"

Andrew turned to see what Judy was screaming about.

"*AAAAANT!*" screamed Andrew and Judy.

The shiny black head was right behind them. They could see their reflection in the glittering wall of eyes.

The ant closed its giant jaws around the fluffy cushion they were sitting on. Then it lifted their cushion and began carrying it—and *them!*—toward the anthill.

*meep* . . . "Ant not eat us!" squeaked Thudd.

"What?" Judy hollered. "We're stuck in a

pair of ant jaws and you say the ant isn't going to eat us? I think you've been dipping your antennas into something weird, Thudd!"

*meep* . . . "This farmer ant," said Thudd. "Take care of mealybug."

Thudd pointed to the fluffy cushion underneath them. "Mealybug!"

Judy gasped. "You mean we're sitting on a *bug*?" she said. "It doesn't even move!"

*meep* . . . "Mealybugs not move much," said Thudd. "Ant carry mealybug into anthill. Like farmer take cow into barn! Humans drink milk. Ants eat mealybug poop! People eat bug poop, too! Sweet, sweet, sweet! Stuck to Oody's hands!"

"*EEEEEWWW!*" said Judy. She frantically wiped the sticky white fluff off her hands.

The next second, the ant zipped down into the anthill. It was like going down a chimney. It got dark. Then it got darker. Their noses filled with damp, moldy smells, like an old cellar.

Andrew unhooked the mini-flashlight from his belt loop and snapped it on.

They were in a vast cave. The light fell on hairy white ropes sticking out of the walls.

*meep* . . . "Roots of plants," said Thudd.

Other ants were skittering across the floor of the cave. One of them came up to Andrew and Judy's ant. The ants waggled their antennas at each other.

*meep* . . . "Ants talk with smells! This ant say she find lost mealybug."

Their ant skittered into a dark hole in the wall of the cave. It was another tunnel.

"Cheese Louise!" said Judy. "We're more lost than ever!"

# VERY IMPORT-ANT!

They came out of the tunnel and into a huge room of the cave.

Andrew's eyes grew wide. "Neato mosquito!" he shouted.

Lying in the middle of the room was a monster-sized ant. It was a hundred times bigger than the other ants! It was surrounded by shiny white eggs. Worm-like things wriggled next to the eggs.

Regular-sized ants were climbing among the eggs and worm-like things, touching them with their antennas.

*meep* . . . "That ant queen!" said Thudd. "Queen ant make all ant babies. Ant babies hatch from eggs. Look like worms. Ant queen use smell to rule! Lotsa ants take care of queen and ant babies."

Their ant carried them through the queen's room into another dark tunnel.

Judy moaned. "How are we ever going to get out of here?"

*meep* . . . "Got idea!" said Thudd. He pointed to his antennas. "Thudd make smells like ant. Try make smell that tell ant to take us out!"

Thudd's antennas waggled. Andrew and Judy couldn't smell anything. But their ant

came to a stop and put down the mealybug.

"Oop!" said Thudd. "Wrong smell."

Thudd waggled his antennas again. The ant gently picked up the mealybug and scampered down the tunnel.

*meep* . . . "Try again," said Thudd, waggling his antennas.

This time, the ant's antennas waggled, too. It turned around in the tunnel and began to race toward the queen's room.

In the queen's room, ants were scurrying frantically. Some carried eggs. They were all leaving. Their ant rushed out with the others.

"Holy moly, Thudd!" said Andrew. "What did you tell them?"

"Make big danger smell!" said Thudd.

Andrew saw a dot of light ahead. Their ant was scrambling up the tunnel that led outside. Andrew turned off his flashlight and clipped it back on to his belt loop.

"We've got to get off this ant!" said Andrew.

"Without getting stomped by the other ants," said Judy.

The ant's head popped out of the anthill. Andrew took a big breath of fresh air.

Ants were trailing out into the garden. Andrew and Judy tugged themselves away from the sticky mealybug.

Their ant was skittering over a rock. The ground below was covered with brown teacup-shaped things. They were half the size of the ant, but they were big enough to be swimming pools for Andrew and Judy. At the bottom of each cup were shiny black blobs.

Andrew pointed to the strange cups. "We can jump into one of those. We'll be safe there until the ants go by," he said.

Judy nodded.

*meep* . . . "Okey-dokey," said Thudd, "as long as no rain happen."

"It's sunny!" said Andrew. He jumped off the mealybug. Judy followed.

Andrew and Judy drifted down into one of the cups. They landed on one of the shiny black blobs. It was sticky.

*meep* . . . "Land in cannon fungus," said Thudd.

"*Cannon* fungus?" said Andrew. "Why do they call it *that*?"

"*Aaaaaack!*" they heard Mrs. Scuttle scream. "I'm soaking wet! Drop that water gun *right now,* you little beast!"

"Nuh-*uh*!" Jeremy Snarfless answered loudly. He gave a nasty laugh.

*Splaaaaat!*

A big drop of water splashed into the cannon fungus.

"Oop! Oop! Oop!" said Thudd. "Hang tight!"

The next instant, the blob, with Andrew and Judy and Thudd on top of it, flew out of the cup! They whizzed up through the leaves. It was like riding a rocket!

"*Yaaaargh!*" yelled Andrew.

"*Yeow!*" yelled Judy.

*meep* . . . "*That* why it called cannon fungus," said Thudd. "Black blob filled with baby fungus spores. When cannon fungus get wet, shoot blob into air so baby fungus find place to live!"

"Zip it, Thudd!" hollered Judy.

The little blob paused, then began to fall!

# SO N-EAR, YET SO FAR

The blob plopped onto a bumpy purple place dotted with spiky pollen.

*meep* . . . "Land on daisy petal," said Thudd.

*"Ah-choooooof!"* sneezed Judy.

"Bless oo!" said Thudd.

Andrew tugged himself off the blob and walked to the edge of the petal.

From there he could see most of Mrs. Scuttle's garden. There were lots of people now. Mrs. Scuttle was serving food from a tray.

She was talking to a tall man with knobby knees and bushy eyebrows.

"Oh! Mr. Ditzworth!" she said. "I hope Boot-a-Pest got rid of those nasty bats in your bathroom!"

Mr. Ditzworth shook his head.

"Tsk, tsk," said Mrs. Scuttle. "Don't worry. We'll be back to boot your bats again!"

She pushed her tray toward him. "Have another teensy cheesy sandwich. These have caviar."

Mr. Ditzworth's eyebrows rose. He picked up a sandwich and nodded.

Jeremy Snarfless reached up to the tray. He grabbed a sandwich and sniffed it.

"What's caviar?" he asked.

"Fish eggs!" said Mrs. Scuttle coldly.

"YUCK!" hollered Jeremy.

He pitched the sandwich into the garden. It landed a few feet away from the daisy.

Harley came running over. He snuffled

among the leaves, found the sandwich, and gobbled it down. One of his long ears flopped against a lily. He raised his rear leg and scratched his ear.

"Look!" said Judy. "If we can get him to come over here and scratch his other ear, maybe he'll shake the helicopter out."

"Harley!" yelled Mrs. Scuttle. "Get out of there! Now!"

She rushed toward Harley. Suddenly she wobbled on her high-heeled sandals. The sandwich tray flew out of her hands!

The sandwiches flew into the air. One of them landed beneath the daisy.

"This could be good!" said Judy.

Harley wagged his tail and bounced into the leaves, searching for sandwiches.

The tray hit the fence and clanked to the ground.

*BZZZZZZZ*

Angry buzzing filled their ears. Yellow-and-black-striped insects were flying low above their flower.

*meep* . . . "Yellow jackets!" said Thudd. "Yellow jackets got nest underground. Mrs. Scuttle hit nest with tray. Make yellow jackets angry. Yellow jackets attack!"

Yellow jackets zoomed toward the garden party.

"Duck!" yelled a woman.

"I don't see a duck," said another.

"Yellow jackets!"

Mrs. Scuttle's guests waved their arms and

bumped into each other as they scurried away from the yellow jackets.

*meep* . . . "Rumble, rumble underground!" said Thudd.

"Are you hearing worms again?" asked Judy.

"Noop! Noop! Noop!" said Thudd. "Cicadas comin' out soon, soon, soon, soon! Millions!"

"And here comes Harley!" said Judy.

In an instant, Harley's big black nose was sniffing the top of their daisy.

Judy pushed Andrew down onto the petal. "Stay low!" she said. "I love Harley, but I am not going swimming in dog snot again!"

Harley's nose moved away from the daisy and headed down to the sandwich.

"How do we get Harley to scratch his ear?" asked Andrew.

"Hmmmm . . . ," murmured Judy. "I have an idea. Give me the Drastic Elastic."

Andrew unzipped the secret pocket under his collar and pulled out the Drastic Elastic.

Judy grabbed it. It was incredibly stretchy and had a little cup at each end.

Judy went to the center of the daisy, which looked like a big pincushion. She tied one end of the Drastic Elastic around one of the tall, pin-like parts. She pointed to a thick lily stem on the other side of Harley's head.

"I'm going to throw the other end of the Drastic Elastic around that stem," she said. "When Harley raises his head, the Drastic Elastic will pull our daisy onto his ear. Let's hope he'll want to scratch it!"

Judy squinted at the thick stem. "It's time for my best curveball pitch," she said.

Judy swung her arm. Her tongue touched the top of her lip, as it did when she pitched in Little League. She threw the end of the Drastic Elastic way over Harley's head toward the stem.

It stretched and s-t-r-e-t-c-h-e-d—and caught! The end spun around the stem. Now the Drastic Elastic stretched above Harley's head.

Harley licked his lips and started to raise his head.

Andrew and Judy held their breath.

Harley's head touched the Drastic Elastic and pushed it up. This pulled the daisy toward his furry brown ear!

"*Yes!*" said Andrew.

He and Judy grabbed on to the pin-cushiony part of the daisy as it tilted. The petals and the ear got closer and closer. Finally, they touched!

Harley's ear twitched a little. Then it twitched *a lot*! Harley's hind leg moved toward his ear.

"He's going to scratch!" said Andrew. "Hang on!"

# WHAT'S UP?

Harley started to scratch—and scratch and scratch! With every scratch, the daisy shook as if there were an earthquake.

Thudd pressed the button that made his Goggle Scope flop down over his face screen. The Goggle Scope made faraway things look near, like a telescope.

*meep* . . . "Drewd! Oody!" squeaked Thudd, pointing below. "Look!"

"I don't see anything," said Andrew.

*meep* . . . "Helicopter!" said Thudd.

"Are you sure?" asked Judy.

"Yoop! Yoop! Yoop!" said Thudd.

"We've got to get down there and find it," said Andrew.

He looked at the Drastic Elastic, tangled between the daisy and the lily. "I guess we'll have to leave the Drastic Elastic behind," he said.

They hopped off the petal and floated down to the dirt.

*meep* . . . "That way!" said Thudd, pointing left as they landed.

Next to a huge, round pit, Andrew and Judy saw a glint of silver.

"THE HELICOPTER!" Judy screamed.

Judy and Andrew scrambled over boulders of dirt. They crept among the squirmy, wormy things wriggling through the soil.

When they got to the helicopter, Judy looked it over carefully. There were just a few scratches and a dent on the door.

"It looks okay," said Andrew.

"But will it fly?" said Judy.

She got into the pilot's seat. Underneath the seat was a little magnetic box where her parents kept the key.

"Fasten your seat belt," said Judy.

She turned the key in the ignition. Nothing happened. She checked the fuel. There was enough.

As Judy tried to start the helicopter again, something shook beneath them.

It felt like they were on top of a huge egg about to hatch!

*meep* . . . "Cicadas comin'!" said Thudd.

Judy tried the ignition again. This time she turned the key farther.

*Yaketta yaketta yakketta,* the engine sputtered.

Something *enormous* was coming out of the pit! A huge brown buggy head with bright round red eyes reared up in front of the helicopter.

Andrew turned to see a herd of red-eyed cicadas behind them!

*ROARRRRRRRRR!* The helicopter engine came to life!

The helicopter wobbled. Then it began to rise up between the leaves! It rose above the daisies! It rose above the roses!

Down below, cicadas were covering the ground! Cicadas were crawling up trees! Cicadas were crawling up legs!

*"Erf!"*

*"Eeeeeyiiiii!!"*

*"Noooooooo!"*

From high above the garden, it looked like Mrs. Scuttle's guests were dancing. But they were frantically shaking off bugs.

Judy steered the helicopter over the fence and into her own yard.

"There's the Atom Sucker!" Andrew yelled. He pointed to the porcupine-shaped machine bouncing under a tree.

Long, skinny copper tubes stuck out all over it. There was a fat iron pipe in the front. That was where the shrinking happened. That was where the un-shrinking was supposed to happen, too.

*KAPOCKETA POCKETA POCKETA!* clattered the Atom Sucker.

The copper tubes were twirling and the whole thing was shaking like a washing machine on spin cycle.

"So how can we push the SHRINK lever to UN-SHRINK?" yelled Judy. "This helicopter is lighter than a ladybug." She checked the clock on the control panel. "It's 7:59," she said. "We've got two minutes left to un-shrink."

Andrew scratched his nose. "Um, fly us to the back of the Atom Sucker," he said. "Get us just above the red switch."

The warm June evening was beginning to get dark. Tiny lights flickered on and off in the yard.

*meep* . . . "Fireflies!" said Thudd. "Got lights in behind! Fireflies blink to find mate!"

"Put a sock in it, Thudd!" yelled Judy.

They were hovering above the back of the Atom Sucker. They could see the big red switch. Beside the switch were two marks. The top one was labeled SHRINK. The bottom one was labeled UN-SHRINK. The switch was pushed up to SHRINK.

"Fly closer to the switch!" Andrew shouted.

"What's your plan, Bug-Brain?" Judy asked.

"Don't worry," said Andrew.

Judy gave Andrew that "wait till I get my hands on you" look. But she flew down and hovered above the red switch.

# SCHLOOOOOOORP!

Andrew reached into his pocket and pulled out the bottle of Bug-Goo. He took the top off the bottle, leaned out of the helicopter window, and squeezed.

*Glug, glug, glug!*

Gloppy green drops of Bug-Goo dripped down onto the red switch.

"Better fly higher!" yelled Andrew.

Down below, rivers of insects began streaming into Judy's yard. Cicadas and ants and termites and beetles!

A cloud of flying bugs swirled around the

Atom Sucker! Fleas and flies! Lightning bugs and ladybugs! Mosquitoes and moths and mantises!

Soon bugs were piled a foot high on the red switch! And still more piled on!

Andrew smiled as he watched. "The weight of all of those bugs should push the

SHRINK-

UN-SHRINK-

switch down to the UN-SHRINK setting!" he said.

Suddenly the Atom Sucker stopped jostling and jolting. It was completely still.

Then, under the blanket of bugs, it looked like the tubes were beginning to twirl slowly in the opposite direction. They picked up speed! They zinged around so fast, the bugs got thrown off!

The big iron pipe in the front wagged just as it did when they got shrunk!

"I think it's ready to un-shrink us," said Andrew. "Let's fly to the front of the big pipe."

Judy rolled her eyes. "I think it's ready to shrink us even *more*," she said. "We should just wait for Uncle Al to come get us."

Before Andrew could say anything, a big bug foot slammed into the helicopter's wind-shield.

"Hold on!" screamed Judy. "We're going to crash!"

The helicopter tumbled through the bug-filled air.

*SCHLOOOOOOORP!*

Suddenly Andrew felt as though he were being tickled by monkeys and squashed into a suitcase.

*There's something awful happening in my pants!* thought Andrew.

His legs felt prickly and tickly—and so did everything else!

Andrew opened his eyes. Bugs were crawling all over him! Ants and cicadas were marching up his seat belt. A praying mantis was perched on his knee. They were all normal bug size! And Andrew was back to normal boy size!

Andrew smiled such a big smile, it felt as though his lips stretched all the way around his head.

"This sounds stupid," said Judy. She was

shaking bugs off of her jacket and scooping bugs out of her socks. "But it's great to be big enough to have bugs crawling on me!"

"Yoop! Yoop! Yoop!" said Thudd from Andrew's shirt pocket.

Through the bug-covered windshield of the helicopter, they saw they were in front of the Atom Sucker. The Atom Sucker and the helicopter were just where they were before they got shrunk.

Judy turned off the helicopter engine. She and Andrew unbuckled their seat belts and stepped out into Judy's yard.

The Atom Sucker was quiet.

"Wowzers!" said Andrew. "Someone must have switched off the Atom Sucker!"

"Christopher Columbus on a buttered bagel!" came a familiar voice.

Uncle Al was making a path through the bugs.

"I am *so* happy to see you guys!" said

Uncle Al, wrapping his arms around them. "And don't worry about the Atom Sucker. I unplugged it!"

*Woof!*

Harley bounded over to Judy. She gave him a big hug and kissed him on his wet black nose.

Mrs. Scuttle was right behind Harley.

"Oh, Professor Dubble!" said Mrs. Scuttle. She was blushing. Beetles were hanging from her hair. Termites were creeping out of her dress. Cicadas were crawling over her sandals and up her legs.

"My party is a total disaster. But it's worth it to have a visit from such a famous person! I saw you on television! You were explaining how dolphins started out as cow-like creatures millions of years ago! Who could believe it?"

"Ah, Mrs. Scuttle," said Uncle Al, "Andrew and Judy have even more amazing things to tell. But right now they look very hungry. Pizza, anyone?"

"Yes!" said Andrew and Judy together.

*meep* . . . "Look for water bear?" said Thudd.

"Thudd!" said Uncle Al. "You found a water bear?"

"Yoop!" said Thudd.

"Amazing!" said Uncle Al. "It's getting dark now, but we'll come back tomorrow, if that's all right with you, Mrs. Scuttle."

"Oh, please *do,* Professor Dubble!" said Mrs. Scuttle. She blushed even more. A firefly flew out of her ear.

Uncle Al led the way out of Judy's backyard. "By the way, guys," he said, "I've been working on this new gizmo, the Water Bug. It's for deep-sea expeditions. Maybe you'd like to help me test it? I'm planning to search for the giant squid. No one has ever seen one alive!"

As they walked through Judy's buggy yard, Andrew had a funny thought. *Maybe you <u>can</u> count on bugs to solve your problems!*

STAY TUNED FOR ANDREW'S NEXT BOOK,
WHEN ANDREW, JUDY, AND THUDD BEGIN
A WHOLE NEW ADVENTURE!

# ANDREW LOST
# UNDER WATER!

In stores July 22, 2003

# TRUE STUFF

Thudd knows a lot, and what Thudd says is true! Thudd wanted to tell Andrew and Judy more about the weird stuff in Mrs. Scuttle's garden, but they were getting "bugged." Here's what Thudd wanted to say:

• A fly's mouth looks like a hose. Flies eat by squirting digestive juices onto their food. The juices turn the food into goo. Then the fly sucks up the goo through its hose-mouth!

• If you take a fistful of dirt, you will be holding billions and billions of microscopic animals!

• Animals that are poisonous to eat—like monarch butterflies—are often very brightly colored. These bright colors are a warning to animals looking for a snack.

• Many animals that use poison to capture their food, like snakes and spiders, are colored to blend in with their environment. This helps them sneak up on their prey.

• A parade of fifty water bears would be only an *inch* long! They're little, but they're probably the toughest animals on Earth. If their environment gets too dry, they dry up, too. They turn into little barrel shapes called "tuns." They can survive like this—without eating or drinking—for more than 100 years! They come back to life when they get wet again. Water bears can survive at temperatures above boiling and below freezing!

• Humans and animals breathe in oxygen and breathe out another gas called carbon dioxide. Plants need carbon dioxide to grow. They take it in through "lips" on their leaves called "stomata." Carbon dioxide is made up of carbon and oxygen. Plants use the carbon and puff out oxygen through their stomata.

• Worms don't have eyes or ears or noses. They don't even breathe! The oxygen they need passes through their skin directly into their blood.

• Ants have very tiny brains. But working together, ants can do amazing things. Some ants keep "ranches," where they raise mealybugs and other insects. The ants drink the insects' poop the way we drink milk! Other ants build amazing tent-like shelters out of leaves. They use silk threads to sew the leaves together. The silk threads are produced by baby ants! The adult ants carry the babies from leaf to leaf like portable sewing machines. The adults tap on the babies' heads to get them to spin out sticky thread!

Find out more!

Visit www.AndrewLost.com.

# WHERE TO FIND MORE TRUE STUFF

They're raising families under your finger-nails! They're boogieing across your pizza! They're having a party in your underpants! They're the weirdly wonderful microscopic creatures that inhabit every inch of the Earth, including the ocean and the air. You can see them in these books:

• *MicroAliens: Dazzling Journeys with an Electron Microscope* by Howard Tomb and Dennis Kunkel (New York: Farrar, Straus and Giroux, 1993)

• *Hidden Worlds: Looking Through a Scientist's Microscope* by Stephen Kramer, with photographs by Dennis Kunkel (Boston: Houghton Mifflin, 2001)

- *Yuck! A Big Book of Little Horrors* by Robert Snedden and Steve Parker (New York: Simon and Schuster, 1996)

Do you want to find out more about insects? Look for these books:

- *Micro Monsters: Life Under the Mircroscope* by Christopher Maynard (New York: DK Publishing, 1999)

You can learn a lot about bugs from this book—and it's funny, too!

- *Ugly Bugs* by Nick Arnold (New York: Scholastic, 1998)

Want to see bugs in 3-D? Check out this big, fat book:

- *The Big Book of Bugs!* edited by Matthew Robertson (New York: Welcome Enterprises, 1999)

Turn the page
for a sneak peek at
Andrew, Judy, and Thudd's
next adventure—

# ANDREW LOST
# UNDER WATER!

Available July 22, 2003

# BYE-BYE, HAWAII!

Andrew Dubble looked up through the tall palm trees.

"This reminds me of when we were lost in the dog-hair forest on Harley's nose!" he said.

"*Eeeuw!*" said Judy, his thirteen-year-old cousin. She gave a little shiver. "I don't *ever* want to think about that! Do you *have* to be so irritating on our very last morning in Hawaii?"

Judy tossed her frizzy hair and marched toward the ocean. She kicked up little fountains of beach sand with every step. Andrew followed her.

*meep* . . . "Drewd and Oody gotta pack

now!" came a squeaky voice from Andrew's shirt pocket. It was Thudd, a little silver robot and Andrew's best friend. "Plane leave in three hours!"

"I guess you're right," sighed Judy. "But I just hate to leave."

Their trip to Hawaii had been so much fun. They swam with dolphins and took an amazing helicopter ride over a volcano!

Andrew and Judy were surprised when Judy's parents took them to Hawaii after the mess they got into three weeks ago.

That was when Andrew accidentally shrunk himself, Judy, and Thudd down to microscopic size with the Atom Sucker. They had been snuffled into a dog's nose, flushed down a toilet, carried off by a cockroach, and dragged into an anthill!

Their parents had been a little upset. But most of all, they were proud of the kids for solving the big problem of being very little.

Judy stopped to pick up a shell.

"Before we finish packing," said Andrew, "there's something I've got to show you."

"What?" asked Judy.

"It's a surprise," said Andrew.

Judy looked at Andrew. Her eyes narrowed. "What kind of surprise?" she asked suspiciously. "The last time you surprised me, I ended up swimming in dog snot."

Andrew laughed. "It's a surprise for Uncle Al," he said.

Andrew and Judy's uncle, Alfred Dubble, was a top-secret scientist. His job was so secret, no one knew exactly what he did. He was the one who invented Thudd.

"Uncle Al has this new invention," said Andrew. "But he's been so busy showing us Hawaii, he hasn't had time to finish it. So I've been getting up early every morning to work on it. I'm going to show Uncle Al what I did after breakfast."

"Cheese Louise!" said Judy. "You've been messing around with one of Uncle Al's inventions? He'll have a cow!"

Andrew shook his head. "Uh-uh," he said. "Come on. We'll be back in ten minutes."

Judy rolled her eyes. "I'd better check this out before Uncle Al does," she said.

Andrew led the way down the beach. Huge blue waves were crashing onto the white sand.

"Wowzers!" said Andrew. "Look how high the waves are!"

*meep* . . . "High tide!" said Thudd. "Moon pull big lump of water to this side of Earth!"

They came to a quiet lagoon surrounded by palm trees. A few small boats were anchored there.

Andrew walked up to a garage on the edge of the water. There was a small box in the middle of the door. Andrew talked into the box. "Good golly, Miss Molly," he said.

*Chugga chugga chugga* came a noise from inside the garage. The garage door rolled up slowly.

Andrew stepped inside and flipped on the light.

"*Ta-da!*" he cried.

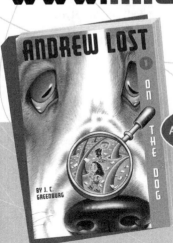

# A STEPPING STONE BOOK™

## Great stories by great authors . . . for fantastic first reading experiences!

### Grades 1–3

FICTION

**Duz Shedd** series
by Marjorie Weinman Sharmat
**Junie B. Jones** series by Barbara Park
**Magic Tree House®** series
by Mary Pope Osborne
**Marvin Redpost** series by Louis Sachar
**Mole and Shrew** books
by Jackie French Koller
**Tooter Tales** books by Jerry Spinelli

**The Chalk Box Kid**
by Clyde Robert Bulla
**The Paint Brush Kid**
by Clyde Robert Bulla
**White Bird** by Clyde Robert Bulla

NONFICTION

**Magic Tree House® Research Guide**
by Will Osborne and
Mary Pope Osborne

### Grades 2–4

**A to Z Mysteries®** series by Ron Roy
**Aliens for . . .** books
by Stephanie Spinner & Jonathan Etra
**Julian** books by Ann Cameron
**The Katie Lynn Cookie Company** series
by G. E. Stanley
**The Case of the Elevator Duck**
by Polly Berrien Berends
**Hannah** by Gloria Whelan
**Little Swan** by Adèle Geras
**The Minstrel in the Tower**
by Gloria Skurzynski

**Next Spring an Oriole**
by Gloria Whelan
**Night of the Full Moon**
by Gloria Whelan
**Silver** by Gloria Whelan
**Smasher** by Dick King-Smith

CLASSICS

**Dr. Jekyll and Mr. Hyde**
retold by Stephanie Spinner
**Dracula** retold by Stephanie Spinner
**Frankenstein** retold by Larry Weinberg

### Grades 3–5

FICTION

**The Magic Elements Quartet**
by Mallory Loehr
**Spider Kane Mysteries**
by Mary Pope Osborne

NONFICTION

**Balto and the Great Race**
by Elizabeth Cody Kimmel
**The *Titanic* Sinks!**
by Thomas Conklin